Judas Maccabaeus by Henry Wadsworth Longfellow

Henry Wadsworth Longfellow was born on February 27th, 1807 in Portland, Maine. As a young boy, it was obvious that he was very studious and he quickly became fluent in Latin.

He published his first poem, "The Battle of Lovell's Pond", in the Portland Gazette on November 17th, 1820. He was already thinking of a career in literature and, in his senior year, wrote to his father: "I will not disguise it in the least... the fact is, I most eagerly aspire after future eminence in literature, my whole soul burns most ardently after it, and every earthly thought centers in it...."

After graduation travels in Europe occupied the next three years and he seemed to easily absorb any language he set himself to learn.

On September 14th, 1831, Longfellow married Mary Storer Potter. They settled in Brunswick.

His first published book was in 1833, a translation of poems by the Spanish poet Jorge Manrique. He also published a travel book, Outre-Mer: A Pilgrimage Beyond the Sea.

During a trip to Europe Mary became pregnant. Sadly, in October 1835, she miscarried at some six months. After weeks of illness she died, at the age of 22 on November 29th, 1835. Longfellow wrote "One thought occupies me night and day... She is dead — She is dead! All day I am weary and sad".

In late 1839, Longfellow published Hyperion, a book in prose inspired by his trips abroad.

Ballads and Other Poems was published in 1841 and included "The Village Blacksmith" and "The Wreck of the Hesperus". His reputation as a poet, and a commercial one at that, was set.

On May 10th, 1843, after seven years in pursuit of a chance for new love, Longfellow received word from Fanny Appleton that she agreed to marry him.

On November 1st, 1847, the epic poem Evangeline was published.

In 1854, Longfellow retired from Harvard, to devote himself entirely to writing.

The Song of Haiwatha, perhaps his best known and enjoyed work was published in 1855.

On July 10th, 1861, after suffering horrific burns the previous day. In his attempts to save her Longfellow had also been badly burned and was unable to attend her funeral.

He spent several years translating Dante Alighieri's Divine Comedy. It was published in 1867.

Longfellow was also part of a group who became known as The Fireside Poets which also included William Cullen Bryant, John Greenleaf Whittier, James Russell Lowell, and Oliver Wendell Holmes Snr.

Longfellow was the most popular poet of his day. As a friend once wrote to him, "no other poet was so fully recognized in his lifetime". Some of his works including "Paul Revere's Ride" and "The Song of Haiwatha" may have rewritten the facts but became essential parts of the American psyche and culture.

Henry Wadsworth Longfellow died, surrounded by family, on Friday, March 24th, 1882. He had been suffering from peritonitis.

Index of Contents

JUDA MACCABAEUS

ACT I

The Citadel of Antiochus at Jerusalem

SCENE I

ANTIOCHUS, JASON.

ANTIOCHUS
O Antioch, my Antioch, my city!
Queen of the East! my solace, my delight!
The dowry of my sister Cleopatra
When she was wed to Ptolemy, and now
Won back and made more wonderful by me!
I love thee, and I long to be once more
Among the players and the dancing women
Within thy gates, and bathe in the Orontes,
Thy river and mine. O Jason, my High-Priest,
For I have made thee so, and thou art mine,
Hast thou seen Antioch the Beautiful?

JASON
Never, my Lord.

ANTIOCHUS
Then hast thou never seen
The wonder of the world. This city of David
Compared with Antioch is but a village,

And its inhabitants compared with Greeks
Are mannerless boors.

JASON
They are barbarians,
And mannerless.

ANTIOCHUS
They must be civilized.
They must be made to have more gods than one;
And goddesses besides.

JASON
They shall have more.

ANTIOCHUS
They must have hippodromes, and games, and baths,
Stage-plays and festivals, and most of all
The Dionysia.

JASON
They shall have them all.

ANTIOCHUS
By Heracles! but I should like to see
These Hebrews crowned with ivy, and arrayed
In skins of fawns, with drums and flutes and thyrsi,
Revel and riot through the solemn streets
Of their old town. Ha, ha! It makes me merry
Only to think of it!—Thou dost not laugh.

JASON
Yea, I laugh inwardly.

ANTIOCHUS
The new Greek leaven
Works slowly in this Israelitish dough!
Have I not sacked the Temple, and on the altar
Set up the statue of Olympian Zeus
To Hellenize it?

JASON
Thou hast done all this.

ANTIOCHUS
As thou wast Joshua once and now art Jason,
And from a Hebrew hast become a Greek,
So shall this Hebrew nation be translated,

Their very natures and their names be changed,
And all be Hellenized.

JASON
It shall be done.

ANTIOCHUS
Their manners and their laws and way of living
Shall all be Greek. They shall unlearn their language,
And learn the lovely speech of Antioch.
Where hast thou been to-day? Thou comest late.

JASON
Playing at discus with the other priests
In the Gymnasium.

ANTIOCHUS
Thou hast done well.
There's nothing better for you lazy priests
Than discus-playing with the common people.
Now tell me, Jason, what these Hebrews call me
When they converse together at their games.

JASON
Antiochus Epiphanes, my Lord;
Antiochus the Illustrious.

ANTIOCHUS
O, not that;
That is the public cry; I mean the name
They give me when they talk among themselves,
And think that no one listens; what is that?

JASON
Antiochus Epimanes, my Lord!

ANTIOCHUS
Antiochus the Mad! Ay, that is it.
And who hath said it? Who hath set in motion
That sorry jest?

JASON
The Seven Sons insane
Of a weird woman, like themselves insane.

ANTIOCHUS
I like their courage, but it shall not save them.
They shall be made to eat the flesh of swine,

Or they shall die. Where are they?

JASON
In the dungeons
Beneath this tower.

ANTIOCHUS
There let them stay and starve,
Till I am ready to make Greeks of them,
After my fashion.

JASON
They shall stay and starve.—
My Lord, the Ambassadors of Samaria
Await thy pleasure.

ANTIOCHUS
Why not my displeasure?
Ambassadors are tedious. They are men
Who work for their own ends, and not for mine
There is no furtherance in them. Let them go
To Apollonius, my governor
There in Samaria, and not trouble me.
What do they want?

JASON
Only the royal sanction
To give a name unto a nameless temple
Upon Mount Gerizim.

ANTIOCHUS
Then bid them enter.
This pleases me, and furthers my designs.
The occasion is auspicious. Bid them enter.

SCENE II

ANTIOCHUS, JASON, THE SAMARITAN AMBASSADORS.

ANTIOCHUS
Approach. Come forward; stand not at the door
Wagging your long beards, but demean yourselves
As doth become Ambassadors. What seek ye?

AN AMBASSADOR
An audience from the King.

ANTIOCHUS

Speak, and be brief.
Waste not the time in useless rhetoric.
Words are not things.

AMBASSADOR [Reading]

"To King Antiochus,
The God, Epiphanes; a Memorial
From the Sidonians, who live at Sichem."

ANTIOCHUS

Sidonians?

AMBASSADOR

Ay, my Lord.

ANTIOCHUS

Go on, go on!
And do not tire thyself and me with bowing!

AMBASSADOR [Reading]

"We are a colony of Medes and Persians."

ANTIOCHUS

No, ye are Jews from one of the Ten Tribes;
Whether Sidonians or Samaritans
Or Jews of Jewry, matters not to me;
Ye are all Israelites, ye are all Jews.
When the Jews prosper, ye claim kindred with them;
When the Jews suffer, ye are Medes and Persians:
I know that in the days of Alexander
Ye claimed exemption from the annual tribute
In the Sabbatic Year, because, ye said,
Your fields had not been planted in that year.

AMBASSADOR [Reading]

"Our fathers, upon certain frequent plagues,
And following an ancient superstition,
Were long accustomed to observe that day
Which by the Israelites is called the Sabbath,
And in a temple on Mount Gerizim
Without a name, they offered sacrifice.
Now we, who are Sidonians, beseech thee,
Who art our benefactor and our savior,
Not to confound us with these wicked Jews,
But to give royal order and injunction
To Apollonius in Samaria.

Thy governor, and likewise to Nicanor,
Thy procurator, no more to molest us;
And let our nameless temple now be named
The Temple of Jupiter Hellenius."

ANTIOCHUS
This shall be done. Full well it pleaseth me
Ye are not Jews, or are no longer Jews,
But Greeks; if not by birth, yet Greeks by custom.
Your nameless temple shall receive the name
Of Jupiter Hellenius. Ye may go!

SCENE III

ANTIOCHUS, JASON

ANTIOCHUS
My task is easier than I dreamed. These people
Meet me half-way. Jason, didst thou take note
How these Samaritans of Sichem said
They were not Jews? that they were Medes and Persians,
They were Sidonians, anything but Jews?
'T is of good augury. The rest will follow
Till the whole land is Hellenized.

JASON
My Lord,
These are Samaritans. The tribe of Judah
Is of a different temper, and the task
Will be more difficult.

ANTIOCHUS
Dost thou gainsay me?

JASON
I know the stubborn nature of the Jew.
Yesterday, Eleazer, an old man,
Being fourscore years and ten, chose rather death
By torture than to eat the flesh of swine.

ANTIOCHUS
The life is in the blood, and the whole nation
Shall bleed to death, or it shall change its faith!

JASON
Hundreds have fled already to the mountains

Of Ephraim, where Judas Maccabaeus
Hath raised the standard of revolt against thee.

ANTIOCHUS
I will burn down their city, and will make it
Waste as a wilderness. Its thoroughfares
Shall be but furrows in a field of ashes.
It shall be sown with salt as Sodom is!
This hundred and fifty-third Olympiad
Shall have a broad and blood-red sea upon it,
Stamped with the awful letters of my name,
Antiochus the God, Epiphanes!—
Where are those Seven Sons?

JASON
My Lord, they wait
Thy royal pleasure.

ANTIOCHUS
They shall wait no longer!

ACT II

The Dungeons in the Citadel

SCENE I

THE MOTHER of the **SEVEN SONS** alone, listening.

THE MOTHER
Be strong, my heart!
Break not till they are dead,
All, all my Seven Sons; then burst asunder,
And let this tortured and tormented soul
Leap and rush out like water through the shards
Of earthen vessels broken at a well.
O my dear children, mine in life and death,
I know not how ye came into my womb;
I neither gave you breath, nor gave you life,
And neither was it I that formed the members
Of every one of you. But the Creator,
Who made the world, and made the heavens above us,
Who formed the generation of mankind,
And found out the beginning of all things,
He gave you breath and life, and will again
Of his own mercy, as ye now regard

Not your own selves, but his eternal law.
I do not murmur, nay, I thank thee, God,
That I and mine have not been deemed unworthy
To suffer for thy sake, and for thy law,
And for the many sins of Israel.
Hark! I can hear within the sound of scourges!
I feel them more than ye do, O my sons!
But cannot come to you. I, who was wont
To wake at night at the least cry ye made,
To whom ye ran at every slightest hurt,
I cannot take you now into my lap
And soothe your pain, but God will take you all
Into his pitying arms, and comfort you,
And give you rest.

A VOICE [within]
What wouldst thou ask of us?
Ready are we to die, but we will never
Transgress the law and customs of our fathers.

THE MOTHER
It is the Voice of my first-born! O brave
And noble boy! Thou hast the privilege
Of dying first, as thou wast born the first.

THE SAME VOICE [Within]
God looketh on us, and hath comfort in us;
As Moses in his song of old declared,
He in his servants shall be comforted.

THE MOTHER
I knew thou wouldst not fail!—He speaks no more,
He is beyond all pain!

ANTIOCHUS [Within]
If thou eat not
Thou shalt be tortured throughout all the members
Of thy whole body. Wilt thou eat then?

SECOND VOICE [Within]
No.

THE MOTHER
It is Adaiah's voice. I tremble for him.
I know his nature, devious as the wind,
And swift to change, gentle and yielding always.
Be steadfast, O my son!

THE SAME VOICE [Within]
Thou, like a fury,
Takest us from this present life, but God,
Who rules the world, shall raise us up again
Into life everlasting.

THE MOTHER
God, I thank thee
That thou hast breathed into that timid heart
Courage to die for thee. O my Adaiah,
Witness of God! if thou for whom I feared
Canst thus encounter death, I need not fear;
The others will not shrink.

THIRD VOICE [Within]
Behold these hands
Held out to thee, O King Antiochus,
Not to implore thy mercy, but to show
That I despise them. He who gave them to me
Will give them back again.

THE MOTHER
O Avilan,
It is thy voice. For the last time I hear it;
For the last time on earth, but not the last.
To death it bids defiance and to torture.
It sounds to me as from another world,
And makes the petty miseries of this
Seem unto me as naught, and less than naught.
Farewell, my Avilan; nay, I should say
Welcome, my Avilan; for I am dead
Before thee. I am waiting for the others.
Why do they linger?

FOURTH VOICE [Within]
It is good, O King,
Being put to death by men, to look for hope
From God, to be raised up again by him.
But thou—no resurrection shalt thou have
To life hereafter.

THE MOTHER
Four! already four!
Three are still living; nay, they all are living,
Half here, half there. Make haste, Antiochus,
To reunite us; for the sword that cleaves
These miserable bodies makes a door
Through which our souls, impatient of release,

Rush to each other's arms.

FIFTH VOICE [Within]
Thou hast the power;
Thou doest what thou wilt. Abide awhile,
And thou shalt see the power of God, and how
He will torment thee and thy seed.

THE MOTHER
O hasten;
Why dost thou pause? Thou who hast slain already
So many Hebrew women, and hast hung
Their murdered infants round their necks, slay me,
For I too am a woman, and these boys
Are mine. Make haste to slay us all,
And hang my lifeless babes about my neck.

SIXTH VOICE [Within]
Think not,
Antiochus, that takest in hand
To strive against the God of Israel,
Thou shalt escape unpunished, for his wrath
Shall overtake thee and thy bloody house.

THE MOTHER
One more, my Sirion, and then all is ended.
Having put all to bed, then in my turn
I will lie down and sleep as sound as they.
My Sirion, my youngest, best beloved!
And those bright golden locks, that I so oft
Have curled about these fingers, even now
Are foul with blood and dust, like a lamb's fleece,
Slain in the shambles.—Not a sound I hear.
This silence is more terrible to me
Than any sound, than any cry of pain,
That might escape the lips of one who dies.
Doth his heart fail him? Doth he fall away
In the last hour from God? O Sirion, Sirion,
Art thou afraid? I do not hear thy voice.
Die as thy brothers died. Thou must not live!

SCENE II

THE MOTHER, ANTIOCHUS, SIRION.

THE MOTHER

Are they all dead?

ANTIOCHUS
Of all thy Seven Sons
One only lives. Behold them where they lie
How dost thou like this picture?

THE MOTHER
God in heaven!
Can a man do such deeds, and yet not die
By the recoil of his own wickedness?
Ye murdered, bleeding, mutilated bodies
That were my children once, and still are mine,
I cannot watch o'er you as Rispah watched
In sackcloth o'er the seven sons of Saul,
Till water drop upon you out of heaven
And wash this blood away! I cannot mourn
As she, the daughter of Aiah, mourned the dead,
From the beginning of the barley-harvest
Until the autumn rains, and suffered not
The birds of air to rest on them by day,
Nor the wild beasts by night. For ye have died
A better death, a death so full of life
That I ought rather to rejoice than mourn.—
Wherefore art thou not dead, O Sirion?
Wherefore art thou the only living thing
Among thy brothers dead? Art thou afraid?

ANTIOCHUS
O woman, I have spared him for thy sake,
For he is fair to look upon and comely;
And I have sworn to him by all the gods
That I would crown his life with joy and honor,
Heap treasures on him, luxuries, delights,
Make him my friend and keeper of my secrets,
If he would turn from your Mosaic Law
And be as we are; but he will not listen.

THE MOTHER
My noble Sirion!

ANTIOCHUS
Therefore I beseech thee,
Who art his mother, thou wouldst speak with him,
And wouldst persuade him. I am sick of blood.

THE MOTHER
Yea, I will speak with him and will persuade him.

O Sirion, my son! have pity on me,
On me that bare thee, and that gave thee suck,
And fed and nourished thee, and brought thee up
With the dear trouble of a mother's care
Unto this age. Look on the heavens above thee,
And on the earth and all that is therein;
Consider that God made them out of things
That were not; and that likewise in this manner
Mankind was made. Then fear not this tormentor
But, being worthy of thy brethren, take
Thy death as they did, that I may receive thee
Again in mercy with them.

ANTIOCHUS
I am mocked,
Yea, I am laughed to scorn.

SIRION
Whom wait ye for?
Never will I obey the King's commandment,
But the commandment of the ancient Law,
That was by Moses given unto our fathers.
And thou, O godless man, that of all others
Art the most wicked, be not lifted up,
Nor puffed up with uncertain hopes, uplifting
Thy hand against the servants of the Lord,
For thou hast not escaped the righteous judgment
Of the Almighty God, who seeth all things!

ANTIOCHUS
He is no God of mine; I fear him not.

SIRION
My brothers, who have suffered a brief pain,
Are dead; but thou, Antiochus, shalt suffer
The punishment of pride. I offer up
My body and my life, beseeching God
That he would speedily be merciful
Unto our nation, and that thou by plagues
Mysterious and by torments mayest confess
That he alone is God.

ANTIOCHUS
Ye both shall perish
By torments worse than any that your God,
Here or hereafter, hath in store for me.

THE MOTHER

My Sirion, I am proud of thee!

ANTIOCHUS
Be silent!
Go to thy bed of torture in yon chamber,
Where lie so many sleepers, heartless mother!
Thy footsteps will not wake them, nor thy voice,
Nor wilt thou hear, amid thy troubled dreams,
Thy children crying for thee in the night!

THE MOTHER
O Death, that stretchest thy white hands to me,
I fear them not, but press them to my lips,
That are as white as thine; for I am Death,
Nay, am the Mother of Death, seeing these sons
All lying lifeless.—Kiss me, Sirion.

ACT III

The Battle-field of Beth-Horon

SCENE I

JUDAS MACCABAEUS in armor before his tent.

JUDAS
The trumpets sound; the echoes of the mountains
Answer them, as the Sabbath morning breaks
Over Beth-horon and its battle-field,
Where the great captain of the hosts of God,
A slave brought up in the brick-fields of Egypt,
O'ercame the Amorites. There was no day
Like that, before or after it, nor shall be.
The sun stood still; the hammers of the hail
Beat on their harness; and the captains set
Their weary feet upon the necks of kings,
As I will upon thine, Antiochus,
Thou man of blood!—Behold the rising sun
Strikes on the golden letters of my banner,
Be Elohim Yehovah! Who is like
To thee, O Lord, among the gods!—Alas!
I am not Joshua, I cannot say,
"Sun, stand thou still on Gibeon, and thou Moon,
In Ajalon!" Nor am I one who wastes
The fateful time in useless lamentation;
But one who bears his life upon his hand

To lose it or to save it, as may best
Serve the designs of Him who giveth life.

SCENE II

JUDAS MACCABAEUS, JEWISH FUGITIVES.

JUDAS
Who and what are ye, that with furtive steps
Steal in among our tents?

FUGITIVES
O Maccabaeus,
Outcasts are we, and fugitives as thou art,
Jews of Jerusalem, that have escaped
From the polluted city, and from death.

JUDAS
None can escape from death. Say that ye come
To die for Israel, and ye are welcome.
What tidings bring ye?

FUGITIVES
Tidings of despair.
The Temple is laid waste; the precious vessels,
Censers of gold, vials and veils and crowns,
And golden ornaments, and hidden treasures,
Have all been taken from it, and the Gentiles
With revelling and with riot fill its courts,
And dally with harlots in the holy places.

JUDAS
All this I knew before.

FUGITIVES
Upon the altar
Are things profane, things by the law forbidden;
Nor can we keep our Sabbaths or our Feasts,
But on the festivals of Dionysus
Must walk in their processions, bearing ivy
To crown a drunken god.

JUDAS
This too I know.
But tell me of the Jews. How fare the Jews?

FUGITIVES
The coming of this mischief hath been sore
And grievous to the people. All the land
Is full of lamentation and of mourning.
The Princes and the Elders weep and wail;
The young men and the maidens are made feeble;
The beauty of the women hath been changed.

JUDAS
And are there none to die for Israel?
'T is not enough to mourn. Breastplate and harness
Are better things than sackcloth. Let the women
Lament for Israel; the men should die.

FUGITIVES
Both men and women die; old men and young:
Old Eleazer died: and Mahala
With all her Seven Sons.

JUDAS
Antiochus,
At every step thou takest there is left
A bloody footprint in the street, by which
The avenging wrath of God will track thee out!
It is enough. Go to the sutler's tents;
Those of you who are men, put on such armor
As ye may find; those of you who are women,
Buckle that armor on; and for a watchword
Whisper, or cry aloud, "The Help of God."

SCENE III

JUDAS MACCABAEUS, NICANOR.

NICANOR
Hail, Judas Maccabaeus!

JUDAS
Hail!—Who art thou
That comest here in this mysterious guise
Into our camp unheralded?

NICANOR
A herald
Sent from Nicanor.

JUDAS

Heralds come not thus.
Armed with thy shirt of mail from head to heel,
Thou glidest like a serpent silently
Into my presence. Wherefore dost thou turn
Thy face from me? A herald speaks his errand
With forehead unabashed.
Thou art a spy sent by Nicanor.

NICANOR

No disguise avails!
Behold my face; I am Nicanor's self.

JUDAS

Thou art indeed Nicanor. I salute thee.
What brings thee hither to this hostile camp
Thus unattended?

NICANOR

Confidence in thee.
Thou hast the nobler virtues of thy race,
Without the failings that attend those virtues.
Thou canst be strong, and yet not tyrannous,
Canst righteous be and not intolerant.
Let there be peace between us.

JUDAS

What is peace?
Is it to bow in silence to our victors?
Is it to see our cities sacked and pillaged,
Our people slain, or sold as slaves, or fleeing
At night-time by the blaze of burning towns;
Jerusalem laid waste; the Holy Temple
Polluted with strange gods? Are these things peace?

NICANOR

These are the dire necessities that wait
On war, whose loud and bloody enginery
I seek to stay. Let there be peace between
Antiochus and thee.

JUDAS

Antiochus?
What is Antiochus, that he should prate
Of peace to me, who am a fugitive?
To-day he shall be lifted up; to-morrow
Shall not be found, because he is returned
Unto his dust; his thought has come to nothing.

There is no peace between us, nor can be,
Until this banner floats upon the walls
Of our Jerusalem.

NICANOR
Between that city
And thee there lies a waving wall of tents,
Held by a host of forty thousand foot,
And horsemen seven thousand. What hast thou
To bring against all these?

JUDAS
The power of God,
Whose breath shall scatter your white tents abroad,
As flakes of snow.

NICANOR
Your Mighty One in heaven
Will not do battle on the Seventh Day;
It is his day of rest.

JUDAS
Silence, blasphemer.
Go to thy tents.

NICANOR
Shall it be war or peace?

JUDAS
War, war, and only war. Go to thy tents
That shall be scattered, as by you were scattered
The torn and trampled pages of the Law,
Blown through the windy streets.

NICANOR
Farewell, brave foe!

JUDAS
Ho, there, my captains! Have safe-conduct given
Unto Nicanor's herald through the camp,
And come yourselves to me.—Farewell, Nicanor!

SCENE IV

JUDAS MACCABAEUS, CAPTAINS AND SOLDIERS.

JUDAS

The hour is come. Gather the host together
For battle. Lo, with trumpets and with songs
The army of Nicanor comes against us.
Go forth to meet them, praying in your hearts,
And fighting with your hands.

CAPTAINS

Look forth and see!
The morning sun is shining on their shields
Of gold and brass; the mountains glisten with them,
And shine like lamps. And we who are so few
And poorly armed, and ready to faint with fasting,
How shall we fight against this multitude?

JUDAS

The victory of a battle standeth not
In multitudes, but in the strength that cometh
From heaven above. The Lord forbid that I
Should do this thing, and flee away from them.
Nay, if our hour be come, then let us die;
Let us not stain our honor.

CAPTAINS

'T is the Sabbath.
Wilt thou fight on the Sabbath, Maccabaeus?

JUDAS

Ay; when I fight the battles of the Lord,
I fight them on his day, as on all others.
Have ye forgotten certain fugitives
That fled once to these hills, and hid themselves
In caves? How their pursuers camped against them
Upon the Seventh Day, and challenged them?
And how they answered not, nor cast a stone,
Nor stopped the places where they lay concealed,
But meekly perished with their wives and children,
Even to the number of a thousand souls?
We who are fighting for our laws and lives
Will not so perish.

CAPTAINS

Lead us to the battle!

JUDAS

And let our watchword be, "The Help of God!"
Last night I dreamed a dream; and in my vision
Beheld Onias, our High-Priest of old,

Who holding up his hands prayed for the Jews.
This done, in the like manner there appeared
An old man, and exceeding glorious,
With hoary hair, and of a wonderful
And excellent majesty. And Onias said:
"This is a lover of the Jews, who prayeth
Much for the people and the Holy City,—
God's prophet Jeremias." And the prophet
Held forth his right hand and gave unto me
A sword of gold; and giving it he said:
"Take thou this holy sword, a gift from God,
And with it thou shalt wound thine adversaries."

CAPTAINS
The Lord is with us!

JUDAS
Hark! I hear the trumpets
Sound from Beth-horon; from the battle-field
Of Joshua, where he smote the Amorites,
Smote the Five Kings of Eglon and of Jarmuth,
Of Hebron, Lachish, and Jerusalem,
As we to-day will smite Nicanor's hosts
And leave a memory of great deeds behind us.

CAPTAINS and **SOLDIERS**
The Help of God!

JUDAS
Be Elohim Yehovah!
Lord, thou didst send thine Angel in the time
Of Esekias, King of Israel,
And in the armies of Sennacherib
Didst slay a hundred fourscore and five thousand.
Wherefore, O Lord of heaven, now also send
Before us a good angel for a fear,
And through the might of thy right arm let those
Be stricken with terror that have come this day
Against thy holy people to blaspheme!

ACT IV

The Outer Courts of the Temple at Jerusalem.

SCENE I

JUDAS MACCABAEUS, CAPTAINS, JEWS.

JUDAS
Behold, our enemies are discomfited.
Jerusalem is fallen; and our banners
Float from her battlements, and o'er her gates
Nicanor's severed head, a sign of terror,
Blackens in wind and sun.

CAPTAINS
O Maccabaeus,
The citadel of Antiochus, wherein
The Mother with her Seven Sons was murdered,
Is still defiant.

JUDAS
Wait.

CAPTAINS
Its hateful aspect
Insults us with the bitter memories
Of other days.

JUDAS
Wait; it shall disappear
And vanish as a cloud. First let us cleanse
The Sanctuary. See, it is become
Waste like a wilderness. Its golden gates
Wrenched from their hinges and consumed by fire;
Shrubs growing in its courts as in a forest;
Upon its altars hideous and strange idols;
And strewn about its pavement at my feet
Its Sacred Books, half burned and painted o'er
With images of heathen gods.

JEWS
Woe! woe!
Our beauty and our glory are laid waste!
The Gentiles have profaned our holy places!

[Lamentation and alarm of trumpets.

JUDAS
This sound of trumpets, and this lamentation,
The heart-cry of a people toward the heavens,
Stir me to wrath and vengeance. Go, my captains;
I hold you back no longer. Batter down
The citadel of Antiochus, while here

We sweep away his altars and his gods.

JUDAS MACCABAEUS, JASON, JEWS.

JEWS
Lurking among the ruins of the Temple,
Deep in its inner courts, we found this man,
Clad as High-Priest.

JUDAS
I ask not who thou art.
I know thy face, writ over with deceit
As are these tattered volumes of the Law
With heathen images. A priest of God
Wast thou in other days, but thou art now
A priest of Satan. Traitor, thou art Jason.

JASON
I am thy prisoner, Judas Maccabaeus,
And it would ill become me to conceal
My name or office.

JUDAS
Over yonder gate
There hangs the head of one who was a Greek.
What should prevent me now, thou man of sin,
From hanging at its side the head of one
Who born a Jew hath made himself a Greek?

JASON
Justice prevents thee.

JUDAS
Justice? Thou art stained
With every crime against which the Decalogue
Thunders with all its thunder.

JASON
If not Justice,
Then Mercy, her handmaiden.

JUDAS
When hast thou
At any time, to any man or woman,

Or even to any little child, shown mercy?

JASON
I have but done what King Antiochus
Commanded me.

JUDAS
True, thou hast been the weapon
With which he struck; but hast been such a weapon,
So flexible, so fitted to his hand,
It tempted him to strike. So thou hast urged him
To double wickedness, thine own and his.
Where is this King? Is he in Antioch
Among his women still, and from his windows
Throwing down gold by handfuls, for the rabble
To scramble for?

JASON
Nay, he is gone from there,
Gone with an army into the far East.

JUDAS
And wherefore gone?

JASON
I know not. For the space
Of forty days almost were horsemen seen
Running in air, in cloth of gold, and armed
With lances, like a band of soldiery;
It was a sign of triumph.

JUDAS
Or of death.
Wherefore art thou not with him?

JASON
I was left
For service in the Temple.

JUDAS
To pollute it,
And to corrupt the Jews; for there are men
Whose presence is corruption; to be with them
Degrades us and deforms the things we do.

JASON
I never made a boast, as some men do,
Of my superior virtue, nor denied

The weakness of my nature, that hath made me
Subservient to the will of other men.

JUDAS
Upon this day, the five and twentieth day
Of the month Caslan, was the Temple here
Profaned by strangers,—by Antiochus
And thee, his instrument. Upon this day
Shall it be cleansed. Thou, who didst lend thyself
Unto this profanation, canst not be
A witness of these solemn services.
There can be nothing clean where thou art present.
The people put to death Callisthenes,
Who burned the Temple gates; and if they find thee
Will surely slay thee. I will spare thy life
To punish thee the longer. Thou shalt wander
Among strange nations. Thou, that hast cast out
So many from their native land, shalt perish
In a strange land. Thou, that hast left so many
Unburied, shalt have none to mourn for thee,
Nor any solemn funerals at all,
Nor sepulchre with thy fathers.—Get thee hence!

[Music. Procession of **PRIESTS** and **PEOPLE**, with cithers, harps, and cymbals. **JUDAS MACCABAEUS**
puts himself at their head, and they go into the inner courts.)

SCENE III

JASON, alone.

JASON
Through the Gate Beautiful I see them come
With branches and green boughs and leaves of palm,
And pass into the inner courts. Alas!
I should be with them, should be one of them,
But in an evil hour, an hour of weakness,
That cometh unto all, I fell away
From the old faith, and did not clutch the new,
Only an outward semblance of belief;
For the new faith I cannot make mine own,
Not being born to it. It hath no root
Within me. I am neither Jew nor Greek,
But stand between them both, a renegade
To each in turn; having no longer faith
In gods or men. Then what mysterious charm,
What fascination is it chains my feet,

And keeps me gazing like a curious child
Into the holy places, where the priests
Have raised their altar?—Striking stones together,
They take fire out of them, and light the lamps
In the great candlestick. They spread the veils,
And set the loaves of showbread on the table.
The incense burns; the well-remembered odor
Comes wafted unto me, and takes me back
To other days. I see myself among them
As I was then; and the old superstition
Creeps over me again!—A childish fancy!—
And hark! they sing with citherns and with cymbals,
And all the people fall upon their faces,
Praying and worshipping!—I will away
Into the East, to meet Antiochus
Upon his homeward journey, crowned with triumph.
Alas! to-day I would give everything
To see a friend's face, or to hear a voice
That had the slightest tone of comfort in it!

ACT V

The Mountains of Ecbatana

SCENE I

ANTIOCHUS, PHILIP, ATTENDANTS.

ANTIOCHUS
Here let us rest awhile. Where are we, Philip?
What place is this?

PHILIP
Ecbatana, my Lord;
And yonder mountain range is the Orontes.

ANTIOCHUS
The Orontes is my river at Antioch.
Why did I leave it? Why have I been tempted
By coverings of gold and shields and breastplates
To plunder Elymais, and be driven
From out its gates, as by a fiery blast
Out of a furnace?

PHILIP
These are fortune's changes.

ANTIOCHUS

What a defeat it was! The Persian horsemen
Came like a mighty wind, the wind Khamaseen,
And melted us away, and scattered us
As if we were dead leaves, or desert sand.

PHILIP

Be comforted, my Lord; for thou hast lost
But what thou hadst not.

ANTIOCHUS

I, who made the Jews
Skip like the grasshoppers, am made myself
To skip among these stones.

PHILIP

Be not discouraged.
Thy realm of Syria remains to thee;
That is not lost nor marred.

ANTIOCHUS

O, where are now
The splendors of my court, my baths and banquets?
Where are my players and my dancing women?
Where are my sweet musicians with their pipes,
That made me merry in the olden time?
I am a laughing-stock to man and brute.
The very camels, with their ugly faces,
Mock me and laugh at me.

PHILIP

Alas! my Lord,
It is not so. If thou wouldst sleep awhile,
All would be well.

ANTIOCHUS

Sleep from mine eyes is gone,
And my heart faileth me for very care.
Dost thou remember, Philip, the old fable
Told us when we were boys, in which the bear
Going for honey overturns the hive,
And is stung blind by bees? I am that beast,
Stung by the Persian swarms of Elymais.

PHILIP

When thou art come again to Antioch
These thoughts will be as covered and forgotten

As are the tracks of Pharaoh's chariot-wheels
In the Egyptian sands.

ANTIOCHUS
Ah! when I come
Again to Antioch! When will that be?
Alas! alas!

SCENE II

ANTIOCHUS, PHILIP, A MESSENGER.

MESSENGER.
May the King live forever!

ANTIOCHUS
Who art thou, and whence comest thou?

MESSENGER
My Lord,
I am a messenger from Antioch,
Sent here by Lysias.

ANTIOCHUS
A strange foreboding
Of something evil overshadows me.
I am no reader of the Jewish Scriptures;
I know not Hebrew; but my High-Priest Jason,
As I remember, told me of a Prophet
Who saw a little cloud rise from the sea
Like a man's hand and soon the heaven was black
With clouds and rain. Here, Philip, read; I cannot;
I see that cloud. It makes the letters dim
Before mine eyes.

PHILIP [Reading]
"To King Antiochus,
The God, Epiphanes."

ANTIOCHUS
O mockery!
Even Lysias laughs at me!—Go on, go on.

PHILIP [Reading]
"We pray thee hasten thy return. The realm
Is falling from thee. Since thou hast gone from us

The victories of Judas Maccabaeus
Form all our annals. First he overthrew
Thy forces at Beth-horon, and passed on,
And took Jerusalem, the Holy City.
And then Emmaus fell; and then Bethsura;
Ephron and all the towns of Galaad,
And Maccabaeus marched to Carnion."

ANTIOCHUS

Enough, enough! Go call my chariot-men;
We will drive forward, forward, without ceasing,
Until we come to Antioch. My captains,
My Lysias, Gorgias, Seron, and Nicanor,
Are babes in battle, and this dreadful Jew
Will rob me of my kingdom and my crown.
My elephants shall trample him to dust;
I will wipe out his nation, and will make
Jerusalem a common burying-place,
And every home within its walls a tomb!

(Throws up his hands, and sinks into the arms of **ATTENDANTS**, who lay him upon a bank.)

PHILIP

Antiochus! Antiochus! Alas,
The King is ill! What is it, O my Lord?

ANTIOCHUS

Nothing. A sudden and sharp spasm of pain,
As if the lightning struck me, or the knife
Of an assassin smote me to the heart.
'T is passed, even as it came. Let us set forward.

PHILIP

See that the chariots be in readiness
We will depart forthwith.

ANTIOCHUS

A moment more.
I cannot stand. I am become at once
Weak as an infant. Ye will have to lead me.
Jove, or Jehovah, or whatever name
Thou wouldst be named,—it is alike to me,—
If I knew how to pray, I would entreat
To live a little longer.

PHILIP

O my Lord,
Thou shalt not die; we will not let thee die!

ANTIOCHUS

How canst thou help it, Philip? O the pain!
Stab after stab. Thou hast no shield against
This unseen weapon. God of Israel,
Since all the other gods abandon me,
Help me. I will release the Holy City.
Garnish with goodly gifts the Holy Temple.
Thy people, whom I judged to be unworthy
To be so much as buried, shall be equal
Unto the citizens of Antioch.
I will become a Jew, and will declare
Through all the world that is inhabited
The power of God!

PHILIP

He faints. It is like death.
Bring here the royal litter. We will bear him
In to the camp, while yet he lives.

ANTIOCHUS

O Philip,
Into what tribulation am I come!
Alas! I now remember all the evil
That I have done the Jews; and for this cause
These troubles are upon me, and behold
I perish through great grief in a strange land.

PHILIP

Antiochus! my King!

ANTIOCHUS

Nay, King no longer.
Take thou my royal robes, my signet-ring,
My crown and sceptre, and deliver them
Unto my son, Antiochus Eupator;
And unto the good Jews, my citizens,
In all my towns, say that their dying monarch
Wisheth them joy, prosperity, and health.
I who, puffed up with pride and arrogance,
Thought all the kingdoms of the earth mine own,
If I would but outstretch my hand and take them,
Meet face to face a greater potentate,
King Death—Epiphanes—the Illustrious!

[Dies.

Henry Wadsworth Longfellow – A Short Biography

Henry Wadsworth Longfellow was born on February 27th, 1807 in Portland, Maine (then part of Massachusetts) to Stephen Longfellow and Zilpah (nee Wadsworth) Longfellow. His father was a lawyer, and his maternal grandfather, Peleg Wadsworth, was a general in the American Revolutionary War and a Member of Congress.

It was a large family. Longfellow was the second of eight children; his siblings were Stephen (1805), Elizabeth (1808), Anne (1810), Alexander (1814), Mary (1816), Ellen (1818) and Samuel (1819).

Longfellow attended a dame school at the age of three and by age six was enrolled at the private Portland Academy. He was very studious and quickly became fluent in Latin. His mother encouraged his love of reading and learning and introduced him to many literary classics.

He published his first poem, a patriotic four-stanza affair entitled "The Battle of Lovell's Pond", in the Portland Gazette on November 17, 1820. He remained at the Portland Academy until he was fourteen. As a child, he spent much of his summers at his grandfather Peleg's farm in the nearby town of Hiram.

In the fall of 1822, the 15-year-old Longfellow enrolled at Bowdoin College in Brunswick, Maine. His grandfather was a founder of the college and his father a trustee. Here he met and befriended Nathaniel Hawthorne. Longfellow was already thinking of a career in literature. In his senior year he wrote to his father: "I will not disguise it in the least... the fact is, I most eagerly aspire after future eminence in literature, my whole soul burns most ardently after it, and every earthly thought centers in it... I am almost confident in believing, that if I can ever rise in the world it must be by the exercise of my talents in the wide field of literature."

Poetry was the writing form he felt most at ease with and he offered poems to many newspapers and magazines. Between January 1824 and graduation in 1825, he had almost 40 poems published, over half of which were in the short-lived Boston periodical The United States Literary Gazette.

When Longfellow graduated, he was ranked a pleasing fourth in the class, and had been elected to Phi Beta Kappa. He was quickly offered the post of professor of modern languages at his alma mater.

Accounts suggest that part of the requirement of acceptance was to tour Europe to become more immersed in both languages and cultures. Longfellow began his tour of Europe in May 1826 aboard the ship Cadmus. His travels in Europe would last three years and cost his father the princely sum of $2,604.24. He visited France, Spain, Italy, Germany and England before returning to the United States in mid-August 1829.

His stock of languages now included French, Spanish, Portuguese, and German, and impressively, mostly without any formal instruction.

On August 27th, 1829, he wrote to the president of Bowdoin that he was turning down the professorship because he considered the $600 salary "disproportionate to the duties required". The trustees countered by raising the salary to $800 and an additional $100 to serve as the college's librarian, a post which required only one hour's attention a day.

On September 14th, 1831, Longfellow married Mary Storer Potter, a childhood friend from Portland. The couple settled in Brunswick. Longfellow now published several non-fiction and fiction prose pieces inspired by his friend Washington Irving, whom he had met in Madrid during his travels, these included "The Indian Summer" and "The Bald Eagle" in 1833.

During his years teaching at the college, he translated textbooks in French, Italian and Spanish; his first published book was in 1833, a translation of the poetry of the medieval Spanish poet Jorge Manrique. A travel book, Outre-Mer: A Pilgrimage Beyond the Sea, was first published in serial form before a book edition in 1835.

In December 1834, Longfellow received a letter from Josiah Quincy III, president of Harvard College, offering him the Smith Professorship of Modern Languages with the condition that he first spend a year or so abroad. The Longfellow's set off for Europe. He would now be able to add German, Dutch, Danish, Swedish, Finnish, and Icelandic to his repertoire of languages.

During the trip they discovered that Mary was pregnant. Sadly, in October 1835, she miscarried some six months into the pregnancy. Then followed several weeks of illness and at the age of 22 on November 29th, 1835 she died. Longfellow had her body embalmed, placed in a lead coffin itself inside an oak coffin which was then shipped to Mount Auburn Cemetery near Boston. He wrote movingly "One thought occupies me night and day... She is dead—She is dead! All day I am weary and sad".

Back in the United States, Longfellow took up the professorship at Harvard. He was required to live in Cambridge, close to the campus and rented rooms at the Craigie House in the spring of 1837. The home, built in 1759, had once been the headquarters of George Washington during the Siege of Boston.

Longfellow now felt able to publish again, starting with the collection Voices of the Night in 1839. It was mainly comprised of translations together with nine original poems and seven poems written back in his teenage years.

His romantic interests also began to surface again. He had begun to court Frances 'Fanny' Appleton, daughter of the Boston industrialist Nathan Appleton. At first, the independent-minded Appleton was not interested in marriage but Longfellow was determined. In July 1839, he wrote to a friend: "Victory hangs doubtful. The lady says she will not! I say she shall! It is not pride, but the madness of passion".

In late 1839, Longfellow published Hyperion, a book in prose inspired by his trips abroad and his still un-successful courtship of Fanny Appleton. Amidst this, Longfellow fell into "periods of neurotic depression with moments of panic" and required a six-month leave of absence from Harvard to attend a health spa in the former Marienberg Benedictine Convent at Boppard in Germany.

Ballads and Other Poems was published in 1841 and included "The Village Blacksmith" and "The Wreck of the Hesperus". His reputation as a poet, and a commercial one at that, was set.

Longfellow published a play in 1842, The Spanish Student, based on his memories from his time in Spain in the 1820s. A small collection, Poems on Slavery, was also published in 1842. This was Longfellow's first public support of abolitionism. However, as Longfellow himself said, the poems were "so mild that even a Slaveholder might read them without losing his appetite for breakfast". The New England Anti-Slavery Association, however, was satisfied enough with the intent of the collection to reprint it for their own distribution.

On May 10th, 1843, after seven years in pursuit, Longfellow received a letter from Fanny Appleton agreeing to marry him. He was elated and immediately walked 90 minutes to meet her at her house.

Nathan Appleton bought the Craigie House as a wedding present to the pair. Longfellow lived there for the rest of his life. His love for Fanny is evident from Longfellow's only love poem, the sonnet "The Evening Star", written in October 1845:

"O my beloved, my sweet Hesperus!
My morning and my evening star of love!"

He once attended a ball without her and said, "The lights seemed dimmer, the music sadder, the flowers fewer, and the women less fair."

Longfellow and Fanny had six children: Charles Appleton (1844), Ernest Wadsworth (1845), Fanny (1847, who died in infancy), Alice Mary (1850), Edith (1853), and Anne Allegra (1855).

Aware of his growing stature and his ability to influence others he also encouraged and supported many other translators. In 1845, he published The Poets and Poetry of Europe, a large 800-page compendium of translated works by other writers. Longfellow intended the anthology "to bring together, into a compact and convenient form, as large an amount as possible of those English translations which are scattered through many volumes, and are not accessible to the general reader".

On November 1st, 1847, the epic poem Evangeline was published.

Longfellow's literary income was now becoming quite substantial: in 1840, he had made $219 but by 1850 it had grown to a very promising $1,900.

On June 14th, 1853, Longfellow held a farewell dinner party at his Cambridge home for his great friend Nathaniel Hawthorne, who was preparing to move overseas.

In 1854, Longfellow retired from Harvard, devoting himself entirely to writing. He would be awarded an honorary doctorate of laws from Harvard in 1859.

The Song of Haiwatha, his epic poem, and perhaps his best known and enjoyed work was published in 1855.

On a hot July 9th day, 1861, Fanny was putting several locks of her children's hair into an envelope and making attempts to seal it with hot sealing wax while Longfellow took a nap. The circumstances of what happened next vary but the actuality is that Fanny's dress caught fire. Her screams awakened Longfellow who rushed to help her and threw a rug over her and stifled the flames with his own body as best he could, but Fanny was already horrifically burned.

A doctor was called and Fanny was taken to her room to recover. She was in and out of consciousness throughout the night and was also administered ether. The next morning, July 10th, 1861, she died shortly after 10 o'clock after asking for a cup of coffee.

Longfellow, in his effort to save her had also been badly burned and was unable to attend her funeral. His facial injuries required he stopped shaving. The ensuing beard now became the quintessential look that everyone remembers from pictures.

Devastated, he never fully recovered and sometimes resorted to laudanum and ether to ease the pain. He worried he would go insane and begged "not to be sent to an asylum" and noted that he was "inwardly bleeding to death". In the sonnet "The Cross of Snow" (1879), which he wrote eighteen years later he wrote:

"Such is the cross I wear upon my breast
These eighteen years, through all the changing scenes
And seasons, changeless since the day she died".

Longfellow spent several years translating Dante Alighieri's epic poem, The Divine Comedy. To aid him in perfecting the translation and reviewing proofs, he invited several friends to weekly meetings every Wednesday from 1864. This became known as the "Dante Club", and regulars included William Dean Howells, James Russell Lowell, Charles Eliot Norton and other occasional guests. The full three-volume translation was published in the spring of 1867, though Longfellow would continue to revise it. It was wildly popular and was re-printed four times in its first year.

By 1868, Longfellow's annual income was over a staggering $48,000.

Longfellow was also part of a group of Poets who became known as The Fireside Poets. The group included Longfellow, William Cullen Bryant, John Greenleaf Whittier, James Russell Lowell, and Oliver Wendell Holmes Snr. Occasionally Ralph Waldo Emerson is also placed among their number. The name "Fireside Poets" derives from poetry reading as a collective family entertainment of the times.

During the 1860s, Longfellow, still a committed abolitionist, also hoped for a coming together, a reconciliation, between the north and south after the dark days of the Civil War. When his son was wounded during the war, he wrote the poem "Christmas Bells", later the basis of the carol I Heard the Bells on Christmas Day.

In 1874, Samuel Cutler Ward helped him sell the poem "The Hanging of the Crane" to the New York Ledger for $3,000; it was the highest price ever paid for a poem. An astonishing sum. But Longfellow was worth it. His fame and audience were widespread and devoted.

Continuing in his hopes for a better and more united America he wrote in his journal in 1878: "I have only one desire; and that is for harmony, and a frank and honest understanding between North and South". Longfellow, despite his aversion to public speaking, took up an offer from Joshua Chamberlain to speak at his fiftieth reunion at Bowdoin College. Here he read the poem "Morituri Salutamus" so quietly that few could hear.

On August 22th, 1879, a female admirer who seemed to know little about his history, traveled to Longfellow's house in Cambridge and, unaware to whom she was speaking, asked Longfellow: "Is this the house where Longfellow was born?" Longfellow told her it was not. The visitor then asked if he had died here. "Not yet", he replied.

Much of Longfellow's work is recognized for its melody-like musicality. As he says, "what a writer asks of his reader is not so much to like as to listen".

Longfellow, like many others of the period, called for the development of high quality American literature. In his work, Kavanagh, a character says: "We want a national literature commensurate with our mountains and rivers... We want a national epic that shall correspond to the size of the country... We want a national drama in which scope shall be given to our gigantic ideas and to the unparalleled activity of our people... In a word, we want a national literature altogether shaggy and unshorn, that shall shake the earth, like a herd of buffaloes thundering over the prairies."

As a translator Longfellow was very impressive. His translation of Dante's The Divine Comedy became a requirement for those who wanted to be a part of high culture.

In 1874, Longfellow oversaw a 31-volume anthology called Poems of Places, collecting poems of several geographical locations; Europe, Asia, and the Arabian countries. It was a work of great educational endeavor but Emerson was disappointed and is said to have told Longfellow: "The world is expecting better things of you than this... You are wasting time that should be bestowed upon original production".

At this point in his life Longfellow could look back and see that his early collections, Voices of the Night and Ballads and Other Poems, had made him instantly popular. The New-Yorker called him "one of the very few in our time who has successfully aimed in putting poetry to its best and sweetest uses". The Southern Literary Messenger immediately put Longfellow "among the first of our American poets".

The rapidity with which American readers embraced Longfellow was unparalleled in publishing history in the United States. His popularity spread throughout Europe, his poems translated into Italian, French, German, and other languages.

Longfellow was the most popular poet of his day. As a friend once wrote to him, "no other poet was so fully recognized in his lifetime". Some of his works including "Paul Revere's Ride" and "The Song of Haiwatha" may have rewritten the facts but became essential parts of the American psyche and culture. He was so admired that on his 70th birthday in 1877 the atmosphere was that of a national holiday, with parades, speeches, and, of course, the reading of his poems.

Over the years, Longfellow's reputation came to include his personality; he was a gentle, placid, poetic soul. James Russell Lowell said, Longfellow had an "absolute sweetness, simplicity, and modesty". The reality was that Longfellow's life was much more difficult than was assumed. He suffered from neuralgia, which caused him constant pain, and poor eyesight. The difficulties of coping with the loss of two wives also took its toll. He was very quiet, reserved, and private; in later years, he became increasingly unsocial and avoided leaving home if he could.

In March 1882, Longfellow went to bed with severe stomach pain. He endured the pain for several days with the help of opium.

Henry Wadsworth Longfellow died, surrounded by family, on Friday, March 24th, 1882. He had been suffering from peritonitis.

He is buried with both of his wives at Mount Auburn Cemetery in Cambridge, Massachusetts. At Longfellow's funeral, his friend Ralph Waldo Emerson called him "a sweet and beautiful soul".

At the time of his death, his estate was valued at $356,320.

In 1884, Longfellow became the first non-British writer for whom a sculpted bust was placed in Poet's Corner of Westminster Abbey in London; he remains the sole American poet thus represented.

Henry Wadsworth Longfellow – A Concise Bibliography

Outre-Mer: A Pilgrimage Beyond the Sea (Travelogue) (1835)
Hyperion, a Romance (1839)
The Spanish Student. A Play in Three Acts (1843)
Evangeline: A Tale of Acadie (poem) (1847)
Kavanagh (1849)
The Golden Legend (poem) (1851)
The Song of Hiawatha (poem) (1855)
The New England Tragedies (1868)
The Divine Tragedy (1871)
Christus: A Mystery (1872)
Aftermath (poem) (1873)
The Arrow and the Song (poem)

Poetry Collections

Voices of the Night (1839)
Ballads & Other Poems (1841)
Poems on Slavery (1842)
The Belfry of Bruges & Other Poems (1845)
The Seaside and the Fireside (1850)
The Poetical Works of Henry Wadsworth Longfellow (1852)
The Courtship of Miles Standish & Other Poems (1858)
Tales of a Wayside Inn (1863)
Birds of Passage (1863)
Household Poems (1865)
Flower-de-Luce (1867)
Three Books of Song (1872)
The Masque of Pandora & Other Poems (1875)
Kéramos & Other Poems (1878)
Ultima Thule (1880)
In the Harbor (1882)
Michel Angelo: A Fragment (incomplete; published posthumously)

Translations

Coplas de Don Jorge Manrique (Translation from Spanish) (1833)
Dante's Divine Comedy (Translation) (1867)

Anthologies

Poets and Poetry of Europe (Translations) (1845)
The Waif (1845)
Poems of Places (1874)

www.ingramcontent.com/pod-product-compliance
Lightning Source LLC
Chambersburg PA
CBHW061506170626
46811CB00004B/1619